Go! Go! Go!

A play by Sally Cowan
Illustrations by Mary Ann Furness

People in the Play

Reader

Mum

Abby
Prue's twin sister

Captain Bell
the fire captain

Prue
Abby's twin sister

Reader

It was late on a cold winter's night.
Abby and Prue were fast asleep
in their bedroom.
But they were woken by a loud noise.

Abby *(sleepily)*

What's that noise?

Prue *(in a scared voice)*

It's the fire alarm.
There must be a fire in the house!

Abby

Oh, no!

Reader

Just then, Mum ran into their bedroom.

Mum

Come quickly, girls!
There's a fire in the bathroom.
We must get out of the house, now!

Abby

Did you call the fire brigade, Mum?

Mum

Yes. Quick! Let's get out!
Smoke is starting to come into the hall.

Prue

We know what to do, Mum.
We have to stay under the smoke.

Abby

Because it can make us sick!
Get down, get low …

Prue

And go, go, go!

Reader

The twins had just had lessons at school
about what to do if a fire started.
They had even talked with Mum
about making their own fire plan at home.
The three of them now got down on the floor,
and crawled down the hallway
towards the door.

Mum

We must stay together, girls!

Reader

Mum and the twins crawled
as quickly as they could to the front door.
More smoke came pouring into the hall.
Mum opened the door.

Mum

Follow me and run to our meeting place,
beside the gate!

Reader

They ran outside to the gate,
just as a fire engine came racing
into their street.

Abby

Here's the fire engine! That was quick!

Prue

And look! There's another one behind it!

Reader

The fire engines screeched to a stop
in front of the house.
Firefighters jumped out
and quickly pulled out fire hoses.
One firefighter ran over to Mum.

Captain Bell

I'm Captain Bell. Is everyone out of the house?

Mum

Yes! There's just the three of us!
The fire is in the bathroom.
Thank you for coming so quickly!

Captain Bell

Now, stay here where it's safe,
and we will put out the fire!

Reader

Mum and the twins stood and watched
as the firefighters worked hard.
After some time, Captain Bell came out
to talk to Mum.

Captain Bell

The fire is out now. But you can't stay here, because the house smells of smoke.
Do you have somewhere else to stay?

Mum

Yes, thank you.
The people next door have phoned my parents.

Abby

Grandma and Grandpa will look after us.

Reader

Weeks went by until, at last,
Mum and the twins could move back
into their house.
Then, one day, a firefighter
came to an assembly at the girls' school.

Prue *(whispering to Abby)*

That's Captain Bell! I wonder why she is here.

Reader

Everyone sat quietly and waited.

Captain Bell

Today, I have awards for two students.
Abby and Prue, please come up onto the stage.

Prue *(looking at Abby)*

Us?

Abby *(surprised)*

But why?

Captain Bell

Abby and Prue, when your house was on fire,
you remembered how to stay safe.
Please tell everyone how you and your mum
got out of the house quickly,
without getting hurt.

Abby

We knew that we had to stay away
from the smoke.
Our teacher had told us to *Get down, get low* …

Prue

And go, go, go!

Captain Bell *(smiling)*

Yes, that's right!
Well done, Abby and Prue!

Reader

Everyone clapped as Captain Bell gave the twins their awards.

Captain Bell

Your mum told me you have moved back into your home.

Abby *(happily)*

Yes. We have a new bathroom now!

Prue

And a new heater that won't start a fire!